*This book is dedicated
to my much loved family,
past, present and future.*

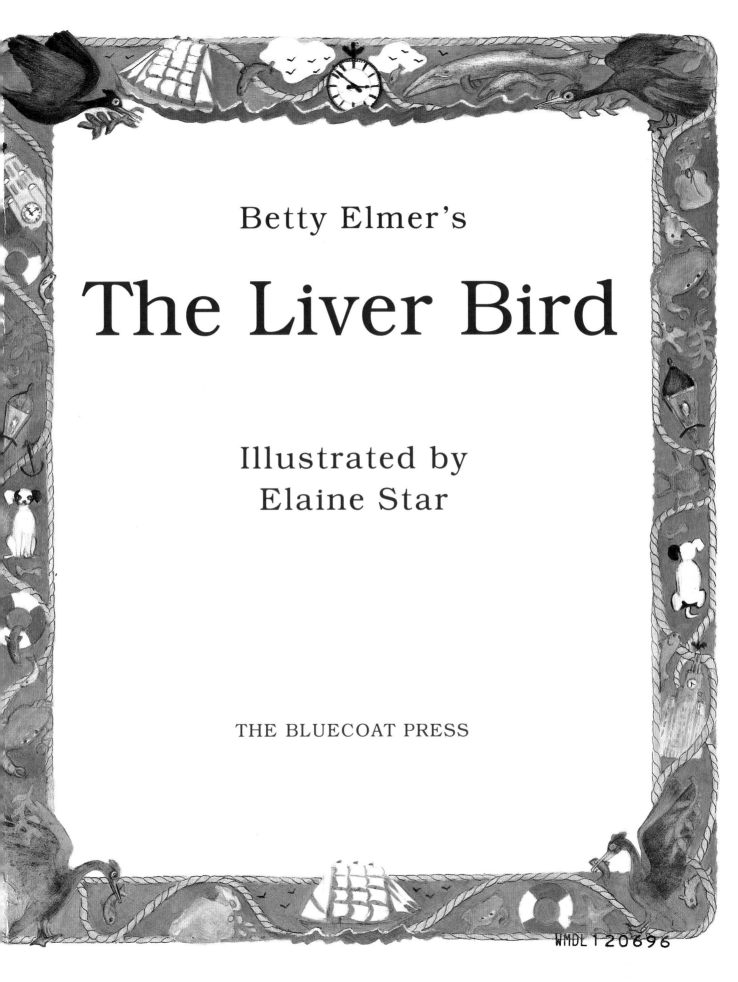

Betty Elmer's

The Liver Bird

Illustrated by
Elaine Star

THE BLUECOAT PRESS

A long time ago in 1911, the Royal Liver Building was being constructed on the Pier Head in Liverpool.

It was the first skyscraper to be built in Britain and would contain no fewer than seventeen floors. On top there were to be two Liver Birds, one facing the city and the other one - the one in our story - facing the River Mersey. From ground level to the top of the Liver Birds, it would measure 322 feet - a wonderful, magnificent creation.

It was to be the splendid new head office of the thriving, prosperous Royal Liver Friendly Society.

It took a small army of workmen to build it - architects, bricklayers and scaffolders to name but a few. They worked and sweated and bent their backs to the task.

Now, amongst all these workmen there was a young lad called Jack. He was fourteen years old and for his first job after leaving school he was working as a builder's mate. One of his tasks was to help fasten the thick sturdy ropes around the great plates of gilded bronze which were being hauled up to create the Liver Bird. These great sections were heaved up to the top and then riveted and screwed into place over a metal frame.

"Haul away" Jack would shout as each enormous bronze plate was pulled skywards. Jack felt that the Liver Bird he had worked so hard to create was his friend.

Then finally
the building work
was finished and on the
19th July 1911 there was a grand
opening ceremony. Everyone of importance was there, the Lord
Mayor, the city councillors, rich merchants, wealthy ship owners and
of course, all the workmen and Jack.

Lord Sheffield, a very important man said "I declare this
building open."

Everyone cheered. It was a great day for Liverpool.

Finally, the ceremony was over. Everyone went home, the Lord Mayor to the Town Hall and Jack to his little house in Brick Street which led off Park Lane near the docks. It was a warm lovely summer evening and he sat on his doorstep munching an enormous jam butty. It was made from a big slice of crusty bread with lashings of butter and thickly spread jam. He also loved chip butties but on this day it was a jam one. As he munched he watched his younger sister playing skipping.

And what nobody could see, not Jack, nor the Lord Mayor, nor Lord Sheffield, was that high up on his tower on top of the Royal Liver Building, the Liver Bird suddenly opened his eyes, stretched his wings and looked around!

What a magnificient view, he could see forever! When he looked straight ahead he could see across the Mersey, past Birkenhead, across the Wirral then across the River Dee to the hills of North Wales. Breathtaking! Over the water, Bidston windmill on Bidston Hill was clearly visible against the evening sky. It was a beautiful, golden sky tinged by the setting sun with apricot, pale green and turquoise, while to the west, the vast expanse of the Irish Sea seemed to have turned into a shimmering cloth of gold.

From the Liver Bird's vantage point, the ships which crowded the busy Mersey and filled the docks stretching along the Liverpool side looked as tiny as floating nut shells. The huge tobacco

warehouse at the Stanley dock
seemed to be no bigger than a very
small shed.

By craning his neck, he could also see
that the city was built on a long low ridge,
a long low hill of sandstone which ran
parallel to the river.

What truly surprised him was the clarity
with which, at a couple of miles distance,
the parish church of St Mary in Walton stood
out against its surroundings. It could be seen
as distinctly as though he was looking at a
village church tower across completely
uninhabited countryside. The Liver Bird could
feel the thrill and the excitement and the
dynamic energy that came from being at the heart
of one of the world's busiest thriving seaports. A
port which was known to travellers and seafarers
the world over.

His sense of glorious freedom and optimism made him
puff out his chest and open his wings wide with
exultation.

"This is my city" he thought with fierce pride
"and I love every single brick!"

Because he was so high up he could
see the coastline curving away to the
north towards Southport and when he
looked down to the mouth of the Mersey, to the
estuary, he could see a number of large black feathered birds. They
had long necks, webbed feet and long powerful bills with a hook on
the end. They were called cormorants, and they were
diving under the water to catch fish. The Liver Bird
gazed with fascination at them.

"We are brothers" he thought. "They are like me, I am like them."
This pleased him greatly.

And then, close by, he spotted Jack, sitting on his doorstep eating
his jam butty watching his sister skipping. The Liver Bird could hear
the hiss of the skipping rope as it cut through the air and the slap as
it hit the cobbles. He could also hear what the little girl was chanting
as she skipped and it was this

> *"What's your name, Mary Jane*
> *Where do you live, down the grid*
> *What number, cucumber*
> *Which house, pan scouse!"*

"How pleased I am" thought the Liver Bird. "I'm in
Liverpool. How marvellous!"

Well, young Jack could not find another job. There was no work in Liverpool, no jobs for anyone, so he decided to go to sea as a cabin boy. He signed on one of the last sailing ships to use the port. She was called the *Liverpool Lady*. One morning in September, Jack's mother stood at the Pier Head, her shawl over her shoulders, waving goodbye. His sisters, with the family dog Raq, were also there, waving and blowing kisses.

The captain was on the foredeck of the *Liverpool Lady*. He called to the first mate, "Mr Mate, weigh anchor, man the capstan and set sail!"

"Aye, aye, sir!" shouted the mate. Then he bawled to the crew "All hands on deck!"

The crew came rushing and stumbling up out of the hold of the ship.

It was the mate's job to make sure that the crew worked very hard.

"Come on lads!" he called to the crew, "man the capstan!" And the crew who were salt encrusted sea dogs, with muscles as big as melons set about the job in hand.

Now a capstan is fastened to the deck, and is like a tall metal drum with a flat wheel on the top, with pigeon holes painted red at regular intervals around the rim. Each crew member took up a wooden handle called a capstan spike, and placed it in one of the holes, so that the handles stuck out from the capstan like the spokes of the wheel. Then each sailor took hold of a handle, and bending double with the effort, started to shuffle round and round, and with each turn of the capstan the anchor chain was wound up and up.

The mate stood by the rail of the *Liverpool Lady* watching every dripping metal link of the chain as it emerged from the muddy waters of the Mersey. Then he shouted to the straining, heaving sailors as they trundled round and round:

"Come on, strike a light! Are you alive or are you dead? Is there a shantyman among you?"

Now a shanty is a work song and one of the crew, the shantyman, immediately sang out
   "Oh say were you never down Rio Grande"
and the crew chorused back
   "Way down Rio!"
then the shantyman called out
      *"Those smart senoritas, they sure
         beat the band"*
         and the crew answered
         "And we're bound for the Rio Grande"

Slowly and surely, the *Liverpool Lady* moved into the middle of the river. As her sails picked up a breeze, and she began to move downstream on a full tide, the sunshine turned the surface of the Mersey into a carpet of twinkling silver stars.

As she made her way down river Jack stood in the

stern of the ship
watching the Pier Head
and the Royal Liver
Building and the
Liver Bird slowly
dwindling in size.
As he gazed
back a shaft of
sunlight caught
the Liver Bird
making him gleam
like gold. Jack felt a
sudden lump in his
throat, he knew that
half of him would feel
homesick while the
other half was filled
with excitement. Who
knows - on this voyage
he might make his
fortune. Suddenly, he
didn't know how or why, into
his head came the words

*"Liver Bird, Liver Bird over the sea,
Liver Bird, Liver Bird come to me"*

He shook his head, "Where did that come from?" he thought.

As the *Liverpool Lady* cleared the mouth of the Mersey, Jack could see the same black, long necked, web footed cormorants that the Liver Bird had spied. They were diving under the water for fish.

"They remind me of the Liver Bird" thought Jack.

His thoughts were broken when the mate called out to the crew:"Right lads, let's give the old town and all our loved ones in her something to remember us by!"

And with great fervour they sang

*"Farewell to Prince's landing stage
River Mersey fare thee well
I am bound for California
A place I know right well*

*So fare thee well, my own true love
When I return united we will be
It's not the leaving of Liverpool that grieves me
But my darling when I think of thee"*

The Liverpool Lady passed the Bar lightship fifteen miles out of Liverpool, cleared the coast of Ireland and set a course for the port of Halifax in a part of Canada called Nova Scotia, which means New Scotland. They were carrying a cargo of molasses out and hoped to return with a cargo of dried fish.

Soon the *Liverpool Lady* was ploughing her way across the wild
wastes of the Atlantic Ocean. Jack had never worked so hard
swabbing down the decks, polishing the mahogany woodwork,
making the brass fittings gleam, helping to set the sails and
swarming up the rigging to keep a look out in the crow's nest at the
top of the main mast.

Now when they were thirty days out of Liverpool and nearing the
coast of Nova Scotia, Jack was in the crow's nest keeping his eyes
skinned for the first glimpse of land. It was very cold, and off the
starboard bow, the right hand side of the ship, he could see several

very large icebergs. Then when he looked out over the port bow, the left hand side of the ship, he could see a huge water spout. It was a whale spouting water out of the blow hole on the top of its head.

"There she blows" Jack cried with great excitement.

A couple of days later the *Liverpool Lady* was sailing into the magnificent natural harbour of Halifax. Passing McNabs Island at the outer extremity of the harbour, they headed for the bustling waterfront and were soon tied up at the quayside.

Jack gazed with excitement at the warehouses and at the fine stone buildings on the busy waterfront. He was thrilled to be soaking up all the sights, sounds and smells of a new country.

"No time for sight seeing" said the mate. "The cargo has to be unloaded with all speed, and the new cargo of dried fish taken on board. We sail on the first tide tomorrow morning. To the owners of the ship, time is money."

Sure enough, by the next morning's tide the new cargo of dried fish was safely stowed in the hold, and the *Liverpool Lady* was heading out of Halifax harbour, bound for Liverpool. Once again Jack was in the crow's nest.

The wind began to freshen, and soon a stiff breeze was billowing out the sails of the ship so that she skimmed along before the wind like a great white bird.

As the wind gusted steadily and increased in strength, the vessel could no longer make any headway and slowly but surely she was blown badly off course.

Then, "Land ho!" shouted Jack.

Ahead was an amazing sight. They were sailing through a wild and desolate stretch of water called The Bay of Fundy. Great steep high cliffs formed the coastline and lining the face of the cliffs, row upon row, were hundreds and hundreds of cormorants. Jack was gazing at them with astonishment when he heard the mate bellow up to him.

"Jack, come down! There's a gale blowing up. You're needed on deck!"

Jack scrambled down the rope ladder and he was just about ten feet above the deck when, in the strengthening wind, the *Liverpool Lady* gave a sudden roll to starboard and Jack lost his grip and plunged overboard into the icy seas.

"Man overboard" yelled the crew.

"Throw him a line" bawled the mate.

The shock of the cold water almost took Jack's breath away, and spluttering and coughing and choking he came to the surface and managed to grab the rope.

"Hold on son!" called the mate, "We'll soon have you in!"

But no matter how hard the crew heaved on the rope they could not pull Jack back on board. His feet had become tangled in some old ropes and rigging that were dangling below the water line.

Jack kicked and struggled frantically but to no avail. His hands were numb and freezing, and he knew that if he didn't free his feet he would soon lose his grip and drown in the icy seas. Then, from nowhere, into his mind came the words

"Liver Bird, Liver Bird over the sea
Liver Bird, Liver Bird come to me"

And, as if in answer to his plea, one of the cormorants left the cliff face and, speeding straight and low like a swift black arrow over the surface of the rough sea, it sped with unerring aim to Jack's side. Then, as though diving for fish, it plunged under the water, and with its powerful beak, it tugged and pulled at the ropes that held him fast until at last he was free.

The crew gave one mighty heave and he was pulled up on to the deck where he lay saturated and waterlogged, gasping and spitting out water.

"It was the bird that set me free" he gasped to the mate. "It was the bird."

"Go below" said the mate "Get yourself into some dry things. The water has

addled your brains."

And at that moment, back in Liverpool, the Liver Bird smiled. He could see over the horizon, right over the curvature of the earth and he knew what had happened.

"Well done, my brother" he silently said to the cormorant.

"Well done, my young friend" he silently said to Jack.

When Jack came back on deck, the sky had darkened and a fierce wind was whistling in the rigging. The crew were furling in the sails, and as they hauled on the ropes they sang

"Windy old weather, stormy old weather
When the wind blows, we all pull together"

When the sails had been taken in, Jack realised that all the crew were gazing upwards at the masts and rigging with expressions of fear and apprehension on their faces. Jack looked up and he too was scared. The masts and all the ropes were covered in an eery, flickering blue-white light. At the top of the main mast there appeared to be a glowing globe of the same white light.

"What is it?" Jack gasped.

"It's called St Elmo's fire" said one of the crew crossing himself.

"It means we are in for a fierce storm".

And so it proved.

The *Liverpool Lady* ran for three tossed and buffeted days and nights before the gale. Waves as high as houses crashed down over the vessel. The wind howled and screamed through the rigging and the boiling sea swept past the ship. Jack was convinced that the *Liverpool Lady* would capsize.

Now sailors are very superstitious, they believe in good luck and bad luck, and at the height of the storm the captain decided that he would toss into the raging seas his valuable silver cuff links as an offering to Aeolus, the King of the Winds, and beg him to make the storm cease.

Carefully he removed the cuff links, and as he threw them overboard he said

"King of the Winds, make the storm cease."

By the next morning, the storm had blown itself out. When the crew looked around they had been blown hundreds of miles off course and seemed to be in another world.

It was dead calm, there was no sign of land, the sea was bright blue, and the sun shone warmly from a cloudless sky. Most noticeable of all was the sea. Floating in it, as far as the eye could see were very broad, very thick, very long matted strands of seaweed. It floated both on and below the surface of the water.

"Where is this place?" whispered Jack.

"It's known as the Sargasso Sea" said the mate.

"We could be becalmed here for weeks. It is said that the wrecks of many good ships are trapped deep down among the seaweed, and that the sound of their ships' bells can be heard when they swing and sway in the water."

Jack could feel his eyes widen.

Every day the sun blazed down on the deck, and in the hot air the sails hung listlessly still.

"You know Jack" said the mate, "I once heard tell that thousands of years ago, a seafarer called Odysseus by some, and Ulysses by others, called at the island belonging to Aeolus, the King of the Winds.

He stayed for a month and when he left, the King of the Winds gave him a leather bag, tied with a silver cord that contained all the winds of the earth except one, the wind called Zephyrus. This was the west wind to blow him home. How I wish we had such a wind!"

As he finished speaking one of the crew jumped to his feet.

"That's all very well" he cried "but where is the wind to blow us back to Liverpool?"

The crew who were bored and restless muttered mutinously among themselves.

"You keep saying we are close to land" continued the sailor. "but can you prove it?"

"Quick Jack" said the mate, "dive into the water. Swim around and see if you can find a crab clinging to the weed. Christopher Columbus was stranded here over four hundred years ago and that is what he did to calm his crew. If you find a crab they will think we are close to land, in fact we are hundreds of miles from shore."

Jack dived into the still warm water and swam slowly amid the great strands of seaweed. Treading water he felt around and to his great joy he did find a crab.

"Look" he shouted to the crew who were leaning over the stern, "a crab! I've found a crab! The mate's right!"

He held the crab high up in the air so that everyone could see it.

Then as his head was bobbing above the water he realised that he could see a cormorant speeding across the dead calm surface of the sea directly towards him.

Instantly, into his head came the words

"Liver Bird, Liver Bird over the sea
Liver Bird, Liver Bird come to me"

The cormorant came to within a couple of yards of Jack and dived below the water. It surfaced with a small bundle in its beak which it

deposited on to the seaweed in front of him. Then it flew away as swiftly as it had arrived. Jack grabbed the bundle and scrambled up a rope ladder on to the deck.

"What have you there?" the mate asked.

Jack looked at the bundle and found he could not speak. He was holding a leather bag tied with a silver cord.

"It's the same bag as in your story" he gasped."No son" said the mate "that story was thousands of years old. There are no winds in this bag."

Jack slowly undid the silver cord and put his hand in the bag. First he pulled out a handful of gold coins, then at the bottom of the bag he could feel a solid object. He reached in and lifted out a small solid gold statue of a cormorant.

The mate was dumbfounded.

"It must be Spanish gold" he said, "thrown overboard hundreds of years ago from a ship caught in a storm. An offering to The King of the Winds to plead for quiet weather."

"Do you realise lads" he called to the crew "it means when we reach Liverpool we'll all be rich."

The crew cheered, and at that moment, back in Liverpool, the Liver Bird smiled. He knew what had happened.

"Well done, my brother" he silently said to the cormorant.

"Well done, my young friend" he silently said to Jack.

"But will we ever reach Liverpool?" asked Jack. "We're becalmed."

"Not for long son, not for long - said the mate. "We're going to whistle up the wind."

"What's that?" said Jack.

"Well" explained the mate, "sailors only whistle on board ship when it's dead calm and a breeze is needed, otherwise it is bad luck. So come along lads, whistle!"

Everyone whistled but not a breath of air stirred.

"Whistle again! Louder! And again, louder still!"

Slowly, imperceptibly, there was a slight movement of air - a shadow of a ripple across the sails.

"One more time" called the mate "whistle for all your worth!"

As if by magic, joyously and majestically the sails billowed and were filled by the rising breeze. The captain gave the command.

"Set a course for home! Set a course for dear old Liverpool!"

Everyone cheered and cheered.

With westerly winds behind her, the *Liverpool Lady* had a swift passage home and soon she was approaching the mouth of the Mersey.

Flags signalling her arrival were hoisted high on poles on Bidston Hill, so that the townspeople of Liverpool, who had thought her lost

at sea, could gather to greet her at the Pier Head.

She glided up to the quayside amid cheers and shouts of greeting. Jack ran down the gangway to give his mother an enormous hug.

There was music and singing and great rejoicing. Everyone joined in and sang a good Liverpool song which went like this

"The big ship sails up the alley alley o
The alley alley o, the alley alley o
Oh the big ship sails up the alley alley o
On the last day of September"

In the middle of all the celebrations Jack stood very still and looked up at the Liver Bird.

"It was all your doing" he thought, "thank you from the bottom of my heart."

And the Liver Bird looked down at Jack and smiled and said silently

"God bless you, my young friend. Wherever you go, and whatever you do, I will always, always be looking after you."

Published by:
The Bluecoat Press
Bluecoat Chambers, School Lane, Liverpool L1 3BX

Design:
Graham Nuttall

Typesetting:
Typebase Ltd

Origination:
Tenon & Polert Colour Scanning

Print:
Printeksa